WEST CHICAGO PUBLIC LIBRARY DISTRICT
3 6653 00278 2781

P9-DHZ-979

TEACH YOUR GIRAFFE TO SKI

VIVIANE ELBEE

PICTURES BY
DANNI GOWDY

Albert Whitman & Company
Chicago, Illinois

To Christine, Tom, Louis, and Pierre—VE

For Alexander & Georgia
with love from Auntie Danni—DG

Library of Congress Cataloging-in-Publication
data is on file with the publisher.

First published in the United States of America
in 2018 by Albert Whitman & Company
ISBN 978-0-8075-7767-7

Printed in China
10 9 8 7 6 5 4 3 2 WKT 22 21 20 19 18

Design by Ellen Kokontis

For more information about Albert Whitman & Company,
visit our website at www.albertwhitman.com.

Uh-oh. It's snowing and your giraffe wants you to teach her to ski.

Offer hot chocolate.

Offer to make snow giraffes.

Offer...

Great spotties! Your giraffe is galloping toward the ski slopes—without skis. Hurry and catch up! She needs you to teach her how to ski safely.

Help your giraffe get her skis on.

Toes in first.

Press down heels.

Snap!

Jumping spotties! She's heading for the Big Scary Slope. Quick! Remind her that *everyone* learns to ski on the bunny hill.
BUNNY HILL

Your giraffe needs to learn how to slow down and stop. Show her how to do a pizza with her skis. (That's the trick to slowing down.)

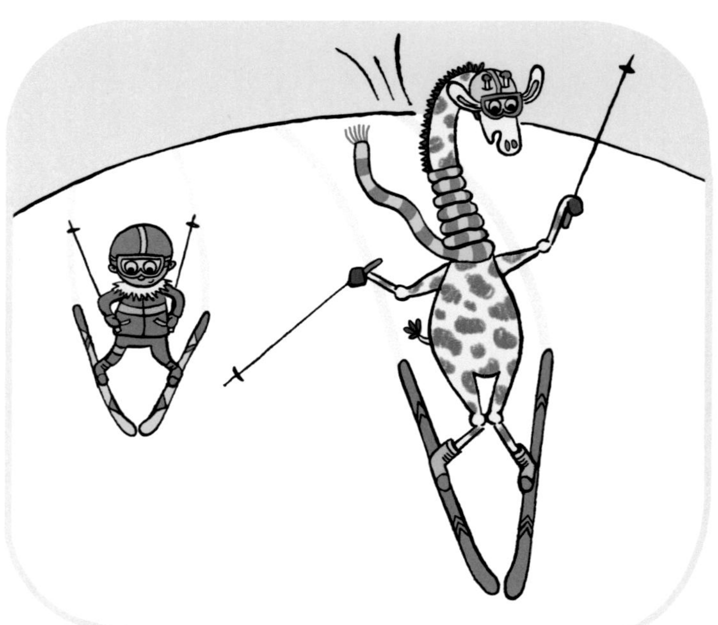

Sometimes skis get tangly.

Time for a break?

No! Your giraffe isn't ready for a break. She wants to go fast.

Show her how to do french fries with her skis. (That's the trick to going fast.)

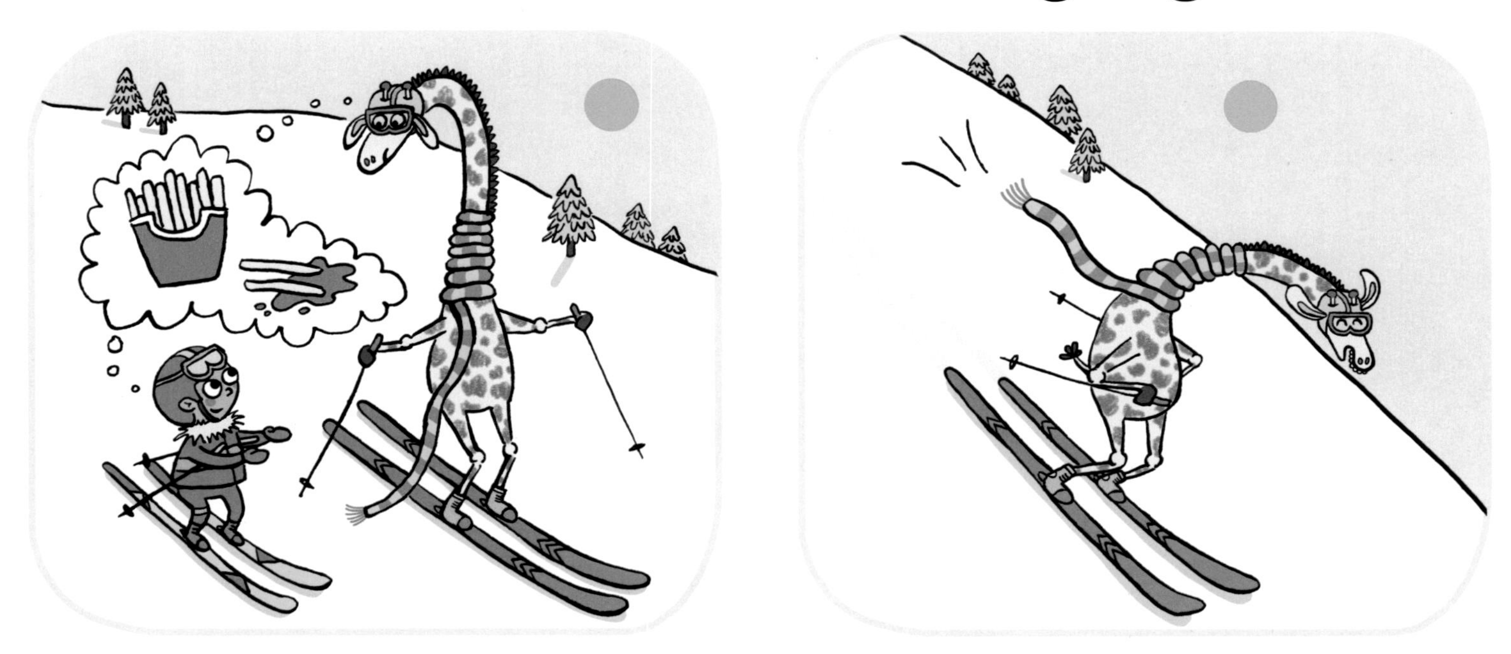

Yikes! Your giraffe is heading for the Big Scary Slope again.

Catch her! Tell her she's ready for the magic carpet that will take her to the tippy top of the bunny hill. The bunny hill is the perfect place to practice.

Pretty soon your giraffe can do great french fries. ZOOM! She's fast. Super fast. A little *too* fast.
Yell, "**Pizza! Pizza! PIZZA!!!!**"

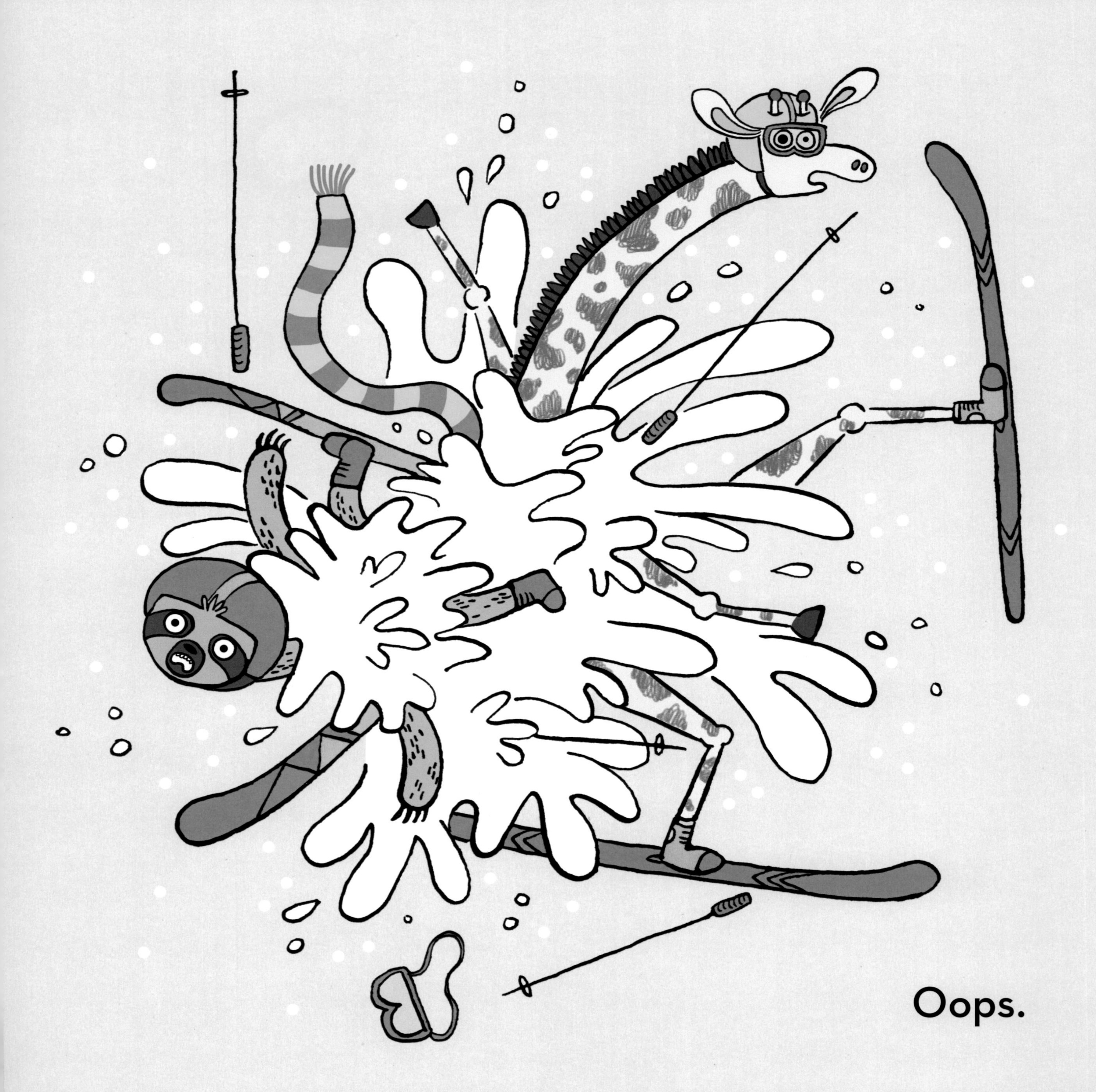

Oops.

Remind her to apologize to the sloth.
Never crash into others. Even if they're slow.

Time for
a break?

No! Your giraffe isn't ready for a break.
She wants to turn.
Show your giraffe how to turn.
Draw S's in the snow with your skis.

Her S's are messy. That's okay. She's learning. She's having fun. She's...

Jumping?!?
Swerving?!?

RACING UP THE
BIG SCARY SLOPE?!?

You have to catch her.
Even if it means riding the SCARY ski lift.

Even if it means getting off on the tippy top of the VERY BIG slope.

Even if it means—

Shooting spotties! You've seen that grin on your giraffe before.

Your giraffe laughs, pushes off and—
she's speeding downhill! Down that
super steep, super long, super SCARY slope!

Stop shaking.

Open your eyes.

Your giraffe *needs* you.
Take a deep breath.

Push off—

Shhhhhhhhhhhhuuuuu...
Wheee!

Maybe your giraffe is right—big hills are FUN!

Uh-oh.
Your giraffe is fast. Super fast. WAY TOO FAST!

SWOOOOOOSH—

KABOOM!

Hug your giraffe to
make her feel better.
Time for a break?

Yes! Your giraffe is ready for a break. She's hungry. She has a serious craving for snow-topped trees. You have a craving for pizza.

Mmm...

Uh-oh. Break time's over.
Your giraffe is heading for the freestyle park. Go, go, go!